I0699814

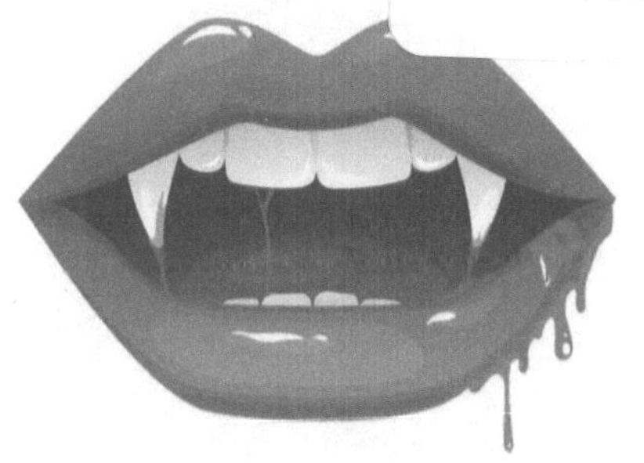

CHOSEN, ETERNALLY

BY

CAROLINE FRANK

Copyright © 2025 by Caroline Frank

All rights reserved.

No part of this book may be reproduced in any form or by any electronic or mechanical means, including information storage and retrieval systems, without written permission from the author, except for the use of brief quotations in a book review.

To the Twilight Girlies.
The Buffy the Vampire Slayer OGs.
The Vampire Diaries fans.
The ones who endlessly debated Team Edward vs. Team Jacob.
Spike vs. Angel.
Damon vs. Stefan.
(There are right answers in this debate, btw)
To all the Sabrina the Teenage Witch fans.
The ones who have been waiting for their magical powers since turning sixteen.
This one's for us.

"Someday, when you're older and wiser, you'll look back on this and get revenge."

— SALEM SABERHAGEN (*SABRINA THE TEENAGE WITCH)*

"I was unconditionally and irrevocably in love with him."

— STEPHENIE MEYER (*TWILIGHT)*

"I would rather spend every moment in agony than erase the memory of you"

— DAMON SALVATORE (*THE VAMPIRE DIARIES)*

"I may be love's bitch, but at least I'm man enough to admit it."

— SPIKE (*BUFFY THE VAMPIRE SLAYER)*

"I'm cookie dough. I'm not done baking. I'm not finished becoming who ever the hell it is I'm gonna turn out to be. I make it through this, and the next thing, and the next thing, and maybe one day, I turn around and realize I'm ready. I'm cookies. And then, you know, if I want someone to eat me—or enjoy warm, delicious, cookie me—then that's fine. That'll be then. When I'm done"

— BUFFY (*BUFFY THE VAMPIRE SLAYER*)

AUTHOR'S NOTE

Hiya!

Thanks for picking up my book!

Before you step into this world, I just wanted to prepare you for what it is: a mini love letter (one of those notes you pass in class, really) to teenage vampire and witchy TV dramas and YA books. Though, obviously for grown-ups because—phew!—does this book have some steamy scenes!!!

It's certainly been a BLAST to write a vampire romance story (honestly, I don't know why I haven't done it before), and maybe this is the start of something new for me, but this book is definitely intended to be a good time novella. Something short and nostalgic. Something for the people who screamed "They should just bang already!" while reading a certain vampire saga.

Anyway, I hope you get a kick out of it. And maybe if I feel like it, it will be the beginning of a saga I'll get to explore more of in the future. Or not. Who knows.

Xo,

Caro

CONTENT WARNING

- Death of parent (off-page)
- Mention of mental illness (off-page)
- Death of family member by suicide (off-page, in past)
- Death of family member by cancer (off-page, in past)
- Very steamy scenes

CHAPTER ONE

The full moon shines bright above James and I where we sit on Proctor's Ledge, making it easy to see every expression on his face when I tell him the news. The location is a bit on the nose for the occasion, but it's hard to live in Salem and not be surrounded by witch culture, no matter who you are.

"Whoa, hold on, Cate. What do you mean you just got this job opportunity you can't tell me about?" he asks, his blond hair nearly white under the stars. He runs his fingers through it, hands that I've imagined so many times over my own body. In the backlight, the sharp lines of his jaw and nose are more pronounced, and the corded muscles of his broad shoulders and arms, even hidden beneath his coat, stand out. I've been struggling with my feelings and attraction for him for a long while, now, and tonight isn't helping. All this setting does is highlight even more just how close to a Greek god James really is—and how far away from one I am. At average height, average body weight, unremarkable face, and ordinary life, anyone who sees us together would stop and wonder what the hell a man like that would be doing with someone like me. And I wouldn't be offended, since I often wonder the same thing.

I twirl a strand of brown hair around my finger. "I know the plan was for us both to quit our current jobs so we can go away together, but... This other thing, it's kind of a big deal."

James is my best friend, and while I'd love to tell him everything, I've been instructed it's the last thing I can do, especially after the sudden way in which the last Protector, Freya, died. The safety of Salem depends on it.

"Does that mean you can't come with me next month? I mean, we've been planning this trip to Asia since freshman year of college, Cate. It's taken nearly a decade to save up all this cash for it, and now you want to cancel?"

"You can still go," I tell him, though I can't hide the pain in my voice. It would break my heart to have him go without me.

James scoffs. "Go without you? The whole point was to go *with* you."

Warmth spreads through me, heating my cheeks despite the cold October night. It isn't even winter yet, but the air is dry and crisp, the promise of an early-season snowfall in the near future.

"I'm sorry, James," I say, my voice cracking. The truth is, I don't want to take on the role as Chosen Protector. I don't want to be Salem's only hope against the vampires.

Don't get me wrong, it's every little witch's dream to be picked to take on this massive role. Who wouldn't want the extra powers the Chosen One receives after the initiation ritual? But the thing is, with the acceptance of these powers comes responsibility, a heavy burden, and a life of near-certain loneliness. Not exactly the qualities you'd see on a job description and make you go, "Yay! I'm totally going to apply!"

And that's the thing, obviously. I didn't *apply* to it. If I had, I'd be called the Selected-From-a-Broad-Pool-of-Candidates One. You can't just submit an application to be considered.

"It was always written, my dear Hecate," I can almost hear my aunt Cybil's voice. *"You were always meant for greatness, and everyone knows it. Still, you can accept or reject it. Though no one in the history of the Society of Witches of Salem ever has."*

But no pressure, right?

So I told the Council Members of The Society that I'd think about it, that there was a chance they'd have to call in an alternate, so to speak.

They weren't big fans of my response.

James sighs, his face the picture of heartbreak.

"I'm sorry," I tell him again.

"It's okay." But it isn't. He looks off into the night, staring up at the full moon without another word. When the silence grows too heavy to bear, he speaks before I can make a run for it: "I wanted this trip to happen. Desperately."

"Me too, but you can still go. You can ask someone else to go with you, if you don't want to go alone. I promise I won't be offended if you—"

"No, Cate, you don't get it." He turns to look at me, a glimmer of desperation and determination in his eyes. "Fuck, I was going to do this on the trip but... I'm done waiting. Done making excuses."

"What are you talking about?"

James takes a deep breath, steeling himself, before taking my gloved hands in his. "Cate, I... I love you. Deeply. *Desperately*. And given how long I've been in love with you, I gather I plan to love you *eternally*. And I know this might be coming out of left field—I'm sorry for that. I guess that's my fault for never being clear about how I feel—though I don't know how I managed to get away with loving you this much without you ever noticing—but I can't keep going like this. It's been ten years and... I know we've both dated other people since then, but these women... they've never been you. I love you, Cate. I love *you*. I *love* you."

"I..." am speechless. Driven mute. Because what does he mean *he loves me*?

"I know I'm an asshole for doing this now. And I promise I'm not doing it to manipulate you into going on this trip. If you need to stay here in Salem, then I'll stay, too. Happily, actually, so long as we're together. And if you don't feel the same way, then..." He shivers, as if the idea that his feelings aren't returned cause more terror in him than any of the evils he doesn't know exist in this very town. "I'll leave. I'll go to Asia on my own and hope to get over you there, and just... I don't know. I'm not sure what I'll do. I was..." He clears his throat and scratches the top of his head. His bare hands are red from the cold, and all I want to do is hold them in mine to warm them up, to protect him.

"Truthfully," he goes on, "I was kind of hoping to have a romantic setting, like the beaches of Bali, for example, to help me out. To tell you how I feel after weeks of bonding over once-in-a-lifetime experiences." James laughs ruefully while I stare at him, mouth agape. "Now that I think about it, it sounds terribly idiotic and—"

I have never seen James this discombobulated. Normally, he's self-assured, confident in a way that reads safety and security rather than arrogance or smugness. He's heart and brains and looks and doesn't know it. Or if he does, he's never once let it get to his head. Not since I've met him, anyway.

"You... love *me*?" I ask for clarification, because I have spent ten years thinking this would never happen for us, and there's no way I can just take his words at face value. I mean, how is this possible?

"Yes," he breathes out, his eyes intense. They lock with mine, and I pray to the gods we stay like this forever. United. Connected. Never apart.

"I love you, too," I manage to say.

James sucks in a breath, those same big blues widening in shock. "Really?" His voice is barely audible, even though it's well past two A.M., and most of the town has been asleep for hours.

I nod slowly, as if in a trance. "Really."

"God, Cate. Can I kiss you?"

CHAPTER TWO

I really must be the Chosen One, because I have been blessed. Knowing that my feelings for James are returned, that he's been as desperate to make us happen as I have for quite some time, is heaven. I no longer feel alone in this. I no longer feel like a fool. More importantly, I can't wait for my new life to begin, with him steadily by my side.

I was already on the precipice of something big—about to pick a life of duty—but this feels bigger. My life doesn't really consist of much besides working day in and day out at my aunt's Magicks Shoppe, training with the Society of Witches on basic skills, and spending my free time with James. It's felt small, almost purposeless.

So it's interesting how one confession from the man I love, one request for a kiss, can tilt my world upside down. Rock it even more than the news that I have been Chosen by some higher power to protect our town from the evil of vampires until the day I die.

My voice is nearly a whisper when I tell him: "Yes, you can kiss me. And I'll turn down the job offer. We can start solidifying our plans for our trip to Asia. Maybe leave as early as next month." The sooner I get away from the judging eyes of The Society and my aunt after I turn down their proposal, the better.

"You don't have to say no to this opportunity. Not if it's something you really want. I told you, I'll stick around for you. You're all I care about, and if this is what you want to do, then I'll—"

"No, no," I cut him off. "*You're* what I want. Us."

"Us," he says with a groan. "I really fucking like the sound of that. Fuck, Cate." James scoots closer to me, our legs dangling over the ledge. He takes my head in his hands, knots his fingers in my hair, and brings my face to his. There's a slight hesitation before our lips touch, but that's okay. After all, there's no doubt this kiss is about to change us and everything about our lives. Regardless of how we feel about each other, we're both smart enough to realize that.

When we finally kiss, it's like nothing I've felt before. His lips are warm despite the weather, and I've never felt safer in my life. When his tongue presses into my mouth, I welcome it, feeling the heat from my cheeks spread all the way down between my thighs. My hands travel up James's chest and lock behind his neck, pulling him closer still to my body. I want every inch of my skin to be pressed up against his.

When I feel one of his hands travel down my shoulder, down my waist, over my thigh, and then back up again under my coat, I shiver—but it isn't because of the winter chill. No, it's the feeling of James's surprisingly warm hand coming over my breast, fitting perfectly in his hand. He cups it while stroking his thumb over my nipple, making me break away and moan out loud in the middle of the night.

James curses under his breath once and whispers, "... can't tell you how fucking long I've been wanting this. How badly I've wanted to love you and kiss you and fuck you."

An electric current shoots up and down my spine at his words, because, my gods, how many times have I had the same thoughts?

"Me too. *Gods*, me too."

I feel James smile against the skin of my neck, press a small bite to it before following it with a kiss. "You and your gods," he says, teasing. "You're the only true goddess."

My laugh comes out breathless because he doesn't even know the half of it. I may not be a goddess, but I was named after one, and were I to accept my role as the Chosen Protector, I'd have near-godlike powers.

Still, James doesn't know that. He accepts my beliefs because he loves me, but he's made it quite clear he doesn't believe in "witch juju." Pretty bold for someone who willingly moved to Salem for college, if you ask me.

I tilt my head back so he can kiss down my neck, but there are too many layers of clothing between us. I wonder idly why he couldn't have confessed his true love earlier in the year, like June or July. Maybe then I could've done something about seeing him topless in his bathing suit on a hot summer day at the beach. You know, instead of replaying a slideshow of images of his muscular body in my head over and over again that very same night while alone in bed.

In the end, it's fine, since this is *sooo* much better than lying under my comforter, my fave vibe in hand, eyes closed as I pant and come to fantasies of James and I breaking through the friend zone. Being in James's arms, his hands roaming my body, moaning into my mouth, truly exceeds expectations—even in below-freezing temperatures.

When James pinches my nipple, the hunger grows too strong—I can no longer keep my head on my shoulders. I am just a few seconds away from using my powers to eviscerate our clothes and beg him to take me out here in the freezing night.

Not that I would mind terribly. Only that I would prefer our first time to be in a more comfortable setting, possibly one where we can avoid getting arrested for public indecency and defacing a historic landmark.

"We need to stop," I tell him as I pull away, though my voice is barely audible over our gasping.

"No, yeah. You're right." James nods, but the expression on his face reveals that he is anything but in agreement. His tongue drags over his bottom lip, his eyes raking over my body. "Or rather, I know you're right *in theory*, but I really don't want you to be."

I laugh and press a kiss against his lips. He doesn't hesitate before wrapping his arms around my waist.

James rests his forehead against mine. "We can go to my place. It's closer."

"Yeah?" I smile, thrilled. With the burden and weight of the decision off my shoulders, and James's confession out in the open, I feel like I could levitate from happiness—which means I should be careful because I could quite *literally* do so if I'm not in control enough of my emotions.

"Yeah." He kisses me again, more intense this time. Sinking into him, I make sure to memorize every detail of this moment. Thanking my powers for my heightened sense of awareness and attention to detail, I know I will forever remember his bergamot and cedar wood scent, the softness of his hair as I run my fingers through it, the warmth of his lips as they move against mine, the eager way his tongue licks into my mouth, the desperate way his hands hold me to him, the moon and stars above, and the snarling noises in the—

Snarling noises? What the—?

CHAPTER THREE

An iron-like vise wraps around my waist and pulls me away from James, throwing me over the ledge. My head hits the concrete when I land, and for a second there, every ounce of oxygen is expelled from my lungs. I can't breathe, can't speak. Can barely think. But once I realize who the mysterious figure—*figures*, plural—who interrupted one of the most religious experiences of my life are, my system kicks into gear. A shot of magic is injected into my veins, my body recovers at an impossible rate, and I'm able to get to my feet in fight mode. I'm not even bleeding.

"*Fucking vampires,*" I mutter right before shooting a Mobilization spell right at the second vamp's chest—a woman with dark, straight hair. She yelps as she flies ten feet in the air and falls with a heavy thud on the grass by a petrified James.

When I run to his side and kneel by him to check whether he's okay, I notice all the color from his face has been drained. And how could it not be, when you just saw your best friend of ten years throw someone through the air without so much as laying a finger on them.

Not sure exactly how I'm going to explain this, but just a minute ago we had confessed our true feelings for each other. This thing with James is real, so I was bound to tell him at one point. This was just… ripping the band-aid. Violently, but still.

"Well, hello there," a tan, five-foot-eight, dark-haired vamp interrupts my musings. If he were a human, he wouldn't look like a particularly threatening man. Just your average Joe, with a runner's body, at most. But I know better. I know just how strong and cunning vampires can be. I know their powers and talents because I've spent countless hours learning about them—even well before I knew it was my destiny to protect this town from them.

"Hey, there." I wiggle my fingers at him, taunting. "Listen, I hate to be *that* girl, but you're kinda cramping my style here. Would you mind coming back, oh…" I tap my index finger pensively to my lip. "I don't know. Maybe never?"

The vamp chuckles darkly. "Yeah, right. Sorry to inconvenience you, but I hear you're the little witch of the hour, Miss Goode. The Chosen One? The '*Protector*?'" He air quotes my new title.

The vamp studies me, his gaze traveling up and down my body as he and his two buddies circle me and James. "We just *had* to come see what the whole fuss was about."

My teasing smile falls. They already know? I haven't even accepted the job, for crying out loud! The news was supposed to be embargoed to the witch community and *definitely* should not have leaked to the fucking *vampires* of all people.

Gods, witches are *such* gossips.

"Cate? What's he talking about?" James asks. All the color has drained from his face, and he looks like he's two seconds away from passing out.

Shit. I need to get James out of here somehow. Unscathed.

"Just... The new job I told you about."

"Why did he call you a witch?"

"I-I don't know." It's a pathetic answer, but it's all I can manage at the moment. I've trained in combat *a bit*, but it hasn't been enough that I can confidently keep up a secret identity *and* battle three vampires while protecting another human. My multitasking abilities aren't *that* developed.

"What do you mean you don't *know*? What's going on? What aren't you telling me?"

Vamp Number Three—tall, dark, devastatingly handsome—sighs dramatically and pinches the bridge of his nose. "Sorry, but can we save the teen show romance drama bullshit for *after* the fight?"

"We're not teenagers," James retorts, somehow offended by this.

"Not really the point, my dude," Vamp Three says.

Well, he isn't wrong.

"Listen, lady and gents," I address them. "Do you mind if I just send my friend here on home? He was just on his way out, and—"

"He *definitely* didn't seem like he was on his way out," Vamp Number Two snickers, her eyes alight with humor. "Maybe we should invite him to our little party here."

With the speed of lightning, I move in front of James and

take a protective stance against these vamps. There's no way I'm going to let them hurt the love of my life.

Over my shoulder, I look at James. "Run as soon as they're all distracted and don't look back," I whisper, too low for the others to hear.

With wide eyes, he panics. "What? *No.* I should be the one defending *you*, not the other way around."

"*No.*" I say it with such finality, he doesn't argue anymore.

When I turn back to face the vamps, I ask "Can we get this over with?" with faux confidence. "I really have some-where to be."

Vamp One snorts. "Alright, then, little witch. Give me your best shot."

I pull my hands to my chest, feet spread apart as I get into position, and cast an Energy spell. While my Protector powers haven't fully settled in yet, I can feel the true strength of the magic building between my hands. A blue ball of energy swirls between us in a mesmerizing glow, so beau-tiful it's hard to believe how deadly it truly is. Once I feel the surge of power reach its limit, I release it, throwing it in the direction of Vamp Number One.

It hits him square in the chest, blasting him through the air, knocking him out of the fight.

There's no way I can help the triumphant smile that spreads across my face—but it's short-lived. Somehow, he gets to his feet and lunges at me, though a little shaken. I brace myself for hand-to-hand combat, but something knocks me on my side taking *me* out this time.

What the hell? There's *no way* he should've survived that

spell. Not even without my powers being fully developed. How did I mess that up? Is he some kind of super vamp, or am I just inadequate?

"Cate!" I hear James call over the ringing in my ears. "I'm gonna fucking *kill* you, you fuckers."

Oh, no.

Deer-legged, I struggle to get to my feet and stop James before he does something stupid, like try to save me. If I weren't so bruised and terrified, I'd almost find it adorable.

"James, no. I have this!"

But it's too late. His body is already mid-flight as he throws himself at Vamp Number Two, who easily wraps two arms around his waist and tackles him to the ground.

"*No!*" I scream. My lungs burn as I push myself to run to his aid. Simultaneously, I begin to cast an Explosive charm to throw at the fucking vampire who dared touch the man I love.

But just when I'm about to release it, just when I'm a few feet away from my love, a blow to the head knocks me unconscious, robbing me of the greatest happiness I could've ever imagined for myself.

CHAPTER FOUR

ONE YEAR LATER...

With the precision of a surgeon, I manage to pick a lock with two bobby pins, eyes closed, hands restrained behind my back. When I hear the door click open, a smirk spreads across my face.

Easy peasy.

"No one likes a sore winner, Hecate," Ian—my Handler—grumbles.

I open my eyes and use my magic to release my hands from the restraints. Ian balks, because they were *supposed* to be magically restrained. However, I think it's time he accepted the fact that his powers are nothing against mine. I mean, it's been nearly a year since the Chosen Protector ceremony gave me a boost in powers. Powers that probably could've saved—

I squeeze my eyes shut, not wanting to think about it now. I'll save it for later tonight, for when I visit him in my dreams.

"I'm not a sore winner; I'm a *bored* winner. When are you going to give me something harder to work on?" It's been a year of training, and while I definitely didn't want the job when it was offered to me, I quickly changed my mind when those three vampires killed the love of my life. To say heartbreak, grief, devastation, and revenge were great motivators would be an understatement. After the funeral (closed casket, of course, because I can't even begin to imagine what those disgusting vamps did to James), I didn't hesitate in assuming the role. I never questioned my destiny again. I was going to defend this town and the world from every single vampire, take them to extinction, dedicate my entire life to it, even if it would never make up for the failure that was losing the world's most precious person.

"I *have* been giving you difficult things. At least according to the curriculum."

"The *curriculum* is ancient."

Ian rolls his eyes at me, the thick lenses of his glasses make it even more comedic, almost cartoonish.

"The curriculum was developed in conjunction with some of the most powerful witches of our coven who gave their lives to protect our kind. The Four surrendered their lives, their powers, and their entire future for every single member of our community. Were it not for them, the humans would have exterminated us back during the Trials."

Now it's *my* turn to roll my eyes at him. "I wasn't saying anything bad about the Four. You always take things so personally. All I meant is that the world is a completely different place than it was in the seventeenth century, for crying out loud."

"Obviously."

"So can we just find a way to update the curriculum?

Focus more on developing strength and technique over dumb stuff like picking locks? I mean, vampires don't even live in places with locks. They live in nests near graveyards. Abandoned warehouses. They don't bother with that kind of security. I need more."

Ian sighs, pinching the bridge of his nose as he squeezes his eyes shut in that frustrated way he always does when he knows I'm making sense but won't admit it.

Men.

"Your powers are strong enough," he grumbles, probably jealous.

I scoff.

"Hecate—"

"Cate."

He narrows his eyes at me. "*He-ca-te,*" he says, enunciating every syllable. "I'm not going to call you by the bastardization of the name of one of the most powerful witches of all time. You were honored with that name. Accept it. Carry it with pride."

"Jesus," I sigh, running my fingers through my hair.

"Hecate," he starts again. "You know that the current political climate in Salem is more unstable than it's ever been. At least since the Trials. Our treaty is up for reevaluation and renewal in January, and with this upcoming mayoral election next month, we may lose everything. Noah Cooke is likely to win, and he is *not* a fan of witches and witchcraft. After William Thacker screwed the pooch with that whole prostitution scandal, he isn't getting reelected. And Cooke has made it clear that, despite the fact that Salem's economy depends largely on tourism in the fall months, he wants the town to stop focusing so heavily on what he calls 'witch culture.' How do you think he's going to react when he's elected into office and the current mayor catches him up on our confidential treaty during the transition period? When he tells him that witches actually *do* exist? What do you think will happen if we step a toe out of line? If he so much as thinks we're a threat, it will be like the Salem Witch Trials Part II. Except this time, the humans have *real* weapons on their sides. It won't matter that we've been keeping the town safe from the vampires all these years."

I sigh and get to my feet. Walk over to his office window to look out onto Salem College's campus where Ian is a professor of Criminology Studies. He also serves as one of Salem's pathologists in the Office of the Chief Medical Examiner—which comes in super handy when hiding vampire-related deaths.

"I understand that we're in a pickle, here, but I think you're losing sight of the fact that the humans aren't the only ones with improved weaponry. May I remind you that vampires don't just use their teeth or superhuman strength anymore? That on top of their powers of Subjugation, they, too, have decided to start using actual weapons?"

Ian gasps so loudly, I turn.

"What do you mean?"

"I *told* you. The vamps last night had actual guns."

"I thought you were joking."

"Why the hell would I be joking about guns?"

"I don't know," he says with a shrug. "Maybe because you tend to be a bit dramatic sometimes."

"Dramatic? When have I ever been dramatic?" I seethe.

He chuckles. "Well, to begin with, that whole thing with that boy was a little bit much, don't you think? You're the Chosen Protector. You need to get used to the occasional casualty, but you were depressed for months. Even your aunt told me she was concerned you were taking it a bit too far."

I narrow my eyes at him, clenching my fists at my side. "I don't believe you. Cybil would never talk about my personal life with you." For months after, she never left my side, offered me a comforting shoulder. My aunt Cybil, who raised me as her own after my mother's suicide and my father's abandonment, never faltered. "Don't you dare try to involve her in this."

He sighs and shakes his head. "That's fine if you don't want to believe me, but she was embarrassed by your moping. And why wouldn't she be? You're supposed to be powerful. Almighty. But you're undeserving if you're going to let a casualty of war bring you to pieces."

Rage shoots through me at an alarming speed, heating the tips of my ears and hands, fingers twitching to do *something*, summon *anything*. To hurt.

I take a deep breath to steady myself before I cast a Fireball spell and burn this whole damn building down with him in it. I don't care if he's my instructor. If Ian is the one who's supposed to guide me. All he's done is lead me down a miserable path I never wanted but only assumed in order to get revenge.

When I feel a little more settled, I speak: "That *boy* was not just a *casualty*. He was the love of my life. Taken from me in the most cruel way imaginable."

Ian rolls his eyes again, and if I hadn't spent the last

twelve months honing my self-control, I would've used my powers to rip them out of his sockets. "See what I mean? Dramatic."

I turn for the door, but he stops me with a hand around my bicep.

"Where the hell do you think you're going? We aren't done here."

I use the fire building in my heart and visualize it, transfer it to my arms and literally burn his palm.

He gasps and shakes his hand as pain spreads through him.

"Don't ever touch me again."

Ian grits his teeth. "You're out of control."

I shrug, nonchalant. "Maybe. But you made me this way." And without another word, I leave, using every ounce of strength inside to walk away with my head held high, holding back tears of grief.

Later that night, I take a bath before I go out hunting for vampires. As I do every time, I turn off the lights, drenching the bathroom in total darkness before turning the ceiling into a moonscape—the same sky from the night they took James: Pegasus and Cassiopeia shine brightest above, along with Perseus's Demon Star—so appropriate for the events that lead to the shaping of the rest of my existence.

I lie back with my eyes closed, and use my mind to call on James, to imagine us back at that very same spot, that very same moment where we confessed our feelings, and imagine different outcomes than the one that actually happened.

Since then, I've dreamed a thousand lives with my love. Tonight will be no different.

Like a catalogue, I sort through different fantasies. Tonight, I decide to fast forward past our confessions last year, all the way to us walking the beaches of Bali under the moonlight (for some reason, I can never imagine us in the daylight)—where we would've ended up had the vampires never taken him from me.

I imagine the cold sand between our toes as he stops to wrap his arms around me and whisper in that deep, molasses-like voice: "You're worth everything, dear Cate. I wouldn't take back those ten minutes of pure bliss for anything in the world."

Even if it's all in my head, the pain in my heart is real. "What are you doing? This is a *fantasy*—you're not supposed to be talking about real things. In here, I imagine what our life should've been like."

He smiles sweetly, fondly. "I think you need this tonight, though. I think you need to hear how happy those last ten minutes of my life made me."

"But you'd still be alive if we never had them. If we hadn't been there, if we'd just stayed home that night—"

"Then there's a chance we might've never admitted how we felt. And it would've meant never having that pure moment of joy. Would you have been able to give it up?"

I swallow thickly, my eyes welling with tears even in my imagination. "I don't know. Maybe? So long as it meant you were alive."

James brings his lips to my ear, his hand raising goosebumps over my skin as he trails his fingers up and down my exposed back.

"I'm still alive. I will always be alive, so long as you continue to live on."

I open my eyes to come back to reality, tears streaming down my cheeks, a hole in my chest yawning open—bigger than the Grand Canyon.

No matter what imaginary James says, my love is gone. The vampires took him away. And nothing will ever change that.

Slowly, I get to my feet in the tub and wave the stars and moonlight away with a sweep of my right hand, summoning a towel with my left.

Fantasy over—it's time to get back to reality.

CHAPTER FIVE

I walk around Gallow's Hill, the gravel crunching beneath my favorite Doc Martens combats, where victims of the Trials are buried in an unmarked mass grave at the base—one of Salem's most famous, after-hours tourist spots, and consequently one of the vamps' favorite hunting grounds.

Mind spinning, I think back to my time with James. How much of it I wasted on my insecurities, on fear. I would vow to never let it happen again, but I don't plan on falling in love with anyone else. Ever. I have enough self-awareness to know that I won't get another love like that. Won't even open myself up to the possibility of it all. But this whole heartbreak has taught me to never let fear stand in the way of what's important. What needs to be done. What is *right*.

Maybe if I'd been brave enough to stand up to The Society, I would've rejected the role of Chosen Protector for Salem, and James and I would've been too busy in Asia, having fun and falling deeper in love, to put ourselves in such a dangerous position. We would've never encountered the vampires.

Or maybe, if I'd been less scared, I would've accepted the

role sooner, gone through the ceremony earlier, and had a boost in powers that would've definitely let us get away scot free from these supernatural killers.

Either way, he'd still be alive today.

You live and you learn. But James didn't. And the vampires won't. Because I'm not going to stop until they're all dead and out of my city. Even if Noah Cooke wins the election and decides to shut magic down. Even if he restarts the modern-day version of the Salem Witch Trials. I won't leave. I will never abandon the people of Salem.

Just when I'm neck deep in vampire murder fantasies, I hear a branch creak behind me. Immediately, adrenaline shoots through my veins, the hairs on the back of my neck rising as my body—and magic—prepare themselves for a fight.

"Here we go," I whisper to myself, getting into position, my long, black leather jacket swishing with the movement.

Looking around, I do my best to find the origin of the sound. Any normal human would think it was innocuous—a fox hunting a mouse, or a bird flying from one branch to another—but I can feel it in my gut: vampires are in the vicinity. More than one, if my powers are correct.

I close my eyes and take a deep breath, concentrating. Three—no, *four* vamps? They're close and getting closer. But I'm ready for them. Ready to take them on.

These days, taking on four vampires feels like a piece of cake. Though they physically outnumber me, their numbers aren't quite enough to overwhelm me into a loss—not without some luck on their end, at least. Even if some have been carrying firearms lately.

Behind me, someone gasps. I turn in place, the end of my high ponytail whipping my cheek. Though I barely notice, because standing across from me is none other than the man who's starred in every single one of my dreams since his supposed death.

"James," I murmur.

His slumped figure is held up by two vampires, each hoisting him by an arm on either side. A third vampire stands beside them, his lips covered in a red liquid.

My nostrils flare at the scent of blood—*James*'s blood.

It's clear from the expressions on their faces that none of them thought they would encounter me tonight. Terror. Fear. They know exactly who I am, and they know they're about to die.

"The Protector," one of them speaks, her voice shaken, yet full of awe.

In this moment, I have no idea what's going on. The image before me leaves me reeling for a moment—but only a short one, because, despite not knowing the details, one thing is for sure: James is alive, he's *here*, and he's in trouble.

Beat vampires to a pulp first, ask questions later, I tell myself.

And that's exactly what I do. I whip my jacket off my shoulders, the cold air biting at my exposed skin, but not distracting enough to pull me away from the task at hand.

I pull my hands to my chest, invoking a Fire Shower spell, a ball of heat and bright orange light building between my palms. After a second, I release it in their direction, the ball splitting into smaller, yet deadly, licks of fire. Each one hits the three vampires squarely in the chest, digging into their clothes until they reach their hearts. In seconds, they scream out in pain and fall to the ground, orange flames enveloping them until they turn to dust.

The whole thing happens so quickly, they barely even notice their own deaths. Part of me almost wishes I'd made it slow, as revenge.

James, who was already semi-conscious, falls to the ground, narrowly avoiding getting burned by the flames beside him. With a swoop of my hand, I stifle the fire to protect him and run to his side.

"James! Is it really you?" I take his hands in mine and gasp. They're cold and paler than usual, but it's him. It's *James*. He's here and he's not dead.

But he's hurt.

His face has nearly been nearly beaten to a pulp, his upper lip broken, blood spilling from the corner of his mouth. I gasp when I see the two teeth marks just over his jugular, my heart sinking in my chest. He isn't dead—somehow hasn't been this entire time—but he could've been if I hadn't been here to save him. His body has been drained of blood, though not in its entirety.

With effort, he opens his blue eyes—beautiful as ever—and whispers, "Cate. Cate, I love you."

James passes out in my arms, and I nearly die of heartbreak.

It takes some serious Invisibility and Levitation charms, but I manage to get James back to my apartment without anyone seeing us. There, I lay him down on the couch and pray to the gods for him to wake.

As I do, I get to work, cooking up a Healing potion for quick recovery. It's something my aunt taught me when I first found my powers—a recipe I've tweaked over the past year to help get me back to 100% after a big fight. It doesn't take long to brew in my pink Dutch oven (cauldrons are *so* seventeenth century), and thankfully revives James seconds after the concoction hits his lips.

"Cate, baby," he whispers, his voice unusually scratchy. Being attacked by a vampire will do that to you, it seems.

"I never thought I'd hear you say my name again," I confess. I have to swallow a hard lump in my throat before I'm able to speak another word. "Please, finish the potion. You'll feel better. And it'll heal your wound."

"My wound?" His brows pull together in an adorable, and oh-so-familiar way.

"Your neck." I point to the bite mark in question.

He brings his hand to the wound, gasping when it comes back with blood.

"I'll get you something to clean that up," I murmur, before getting to my feet to get a first aid kit.

"What happened?" he asks as I dress his wound. Thanks to the potion I gave him, it'll be gone in less than 48 hours. Still, better safe than sorry.

"I should be asking you that." I sniffle, realizing too late that I'm crying. I haven't cried since his funeral.

His *funeral.*

If he's alive, then who the hell were we all mourning in that coffin? Who did we bury in that grave?

I wipe my eyes with the heels of my hands and sit beside him, trembling.

"I don't know." He shakes his head, eyes downcast. "The last thing I remember before being taken is... Well, the conversation we had." He looks up at me, and I want to die. I want to die because he's been alive this entire time and I didn't know. And I could've come and saved him. "Then, I remember a bunch of vampires got to us—which, like, who knew they existed, by the way? Well, I guess you did—and you got knocked out. Then they knocked *me* out, and the next thing I know I'm in some dark basement getting fed under a door. It was like... like something out of a horror movie."

James's eyes are glassy, brimming with tears, but I can't breathe. Because I didn't *know*. I thought he was dead. And all this time he's been suffering, kept in a cage like an animal. The best person I've ever known had to endure that torture for over a year.

I can't even imagine what they did to him.

"Then, out of nowhere, they pulled me from my cell. They didn't say why, but they brought me here for some reason."

"Gods, James," I say with a sob, dropping my face in my hands. "I thought you were dead. You've *been* dead. And now you're telling me you've been alive this entire time? That you've been trapped in hell for over a year?"

"Over a year?" He gasps. "Are you serious?"

I nod.

"Jesus-fucking-Christ. I didn't—" he stutters. "It was so dark in there, I couldn't keep track of time."

"I'm s-so s-sorry." Nothing I do or say will ever be enough. It will never make up for the fact that I abandoned my best friend and the so-called love of my life to fend for himself for over a year with a bunch of vampires. I mean, I'm the godsdamn Chosen Protector! Shouldn't something inside of me have told me he was still here?

"Stop blaming yourself. It wasn't your fault."

"It was. It definitely was."

He presses his lips together, his brows set in that way that tells me he's not budging on this. Still, he says, "It wasn't your fault, Cate. But you do owe me an explanation."

CHAPTER SIX

"Okay, so let me get this straight," James begins his recap. "You've been a witch since before I even met you, but you only had a limited amount of powers then. It wasn't until you became the Chosen Guardian and—"

"*Protector*. Chosen Protector," I correct.

James waves a hand. "Protector, then. It wasn't until you became a Chosen Protector that all these powers developed into something more, and you were sworn in to protect the city of Salem from vampires?"

"Right." I nod. "But the swearing in ceremony kinda didn't happen until after you... Well, until after we thought you died."

He whistles once, shocked. "Okay, then. Well. I have... So many questions."

"Right, I thought you might have a couple."

"Okay, so, first one off the top of my head: I'm clearly not dead," he says with a laugh.

"Not a question."

He shoots me a frustrated look, and I sigh.

"We thought you were dead. Or rather, I did. But only

because that's what I was told after I woke up in the hospital the day after our encounter with those vamps. I went to your funeral and everything, and it was—" Again, I struggle to breathe. To push through the memories of other people grieving James in the small room of the funeral home. Thinking that while they were entitled to be sad, none of them would ever know the true pain of his loss like I would.

It takes a second for me to be able to recover, and when I do, I know I have to be as clear and honest as possible. "Someone lied. Tricked me and the Society into thinking you'd died. Somehow convinced the authorities—the police and the morgue—to lie about the condition your body was left in, and say that it was mangled almost beyond recognition. It's why they told us the wake couldn't be open casket."

James looks at me, devastated.

"I don't know what happened, James. Maybe it was another vampire using their powers of Subjugation? Though we supply city officials with antidotes to protect them from situations just like this. So I'm at a loss. But I promise that we'll go first thing tomorrow morning to The Society and try to sort this whole thing out. Tell them how you were held in a cell for over a year, and just..." I shiver. "I promise if I wasn't already fueled by revenge before, I sure as hell am now."

He half-smiles. "Okay, so I get why you thought I was dead. But can we rewind to the genesis of it all? Like, what the hell are vampires doing in Salem? And why are witches the ones stopping them? Why doesn't the rest of the world know?"

I sigh because this a tough one. "It's kind of a long story. But the TL;DR version of it is that vampire killings started happening around the same time as the Salem Witch Trials —yes, most of the witches executed were *actual* witches, though not all of them. Now, the witches already knew of the existence of this species from their ancestors back in Europe, but the humans didn't. Supposedly, there were no vampires here, but somehow they managed to make it to Massachusetts. We covered up every single vampire death by saying they were 'animal-related,'" I say, recalling my mandatory history lessons from my teenage years.

"One night, there was a town hall meeting happening. Four of the strongest members of our coven were on trial and headed straight for the gallows. Almost a hundred people attended that meeting, which back then, was a lot. Suddenly, over a dozen vampires broke into the town hall and started attacking the humans, ripping their throats out right then and there. Now, for obvious reasons, we had never publicly used our powers in front of humans. The witches back then were adopting a 'deny til you die' philosophy, which they took quite literally, unfortunately. But the Four—Agnes, Mary, Emily, and Elizabeth—refused to stand idly by as people were massacred, even if these people were trying to execute them. So they used their collective powers to kill the vampires who attacked the meeting and ward the rest of them off."

"Jesus," James breathes. "And *that's* the 'too long; didn't read version'?" He laughs, and the sound of it makes my heart soar despite it all.

"I know." I sigh. "It's a lot. In the end, only seven human lives were lost that night. The rest were protected thanks to our fearless leaders. After that, the city of Salem was so thankful that we reached an agreement with the officials: the witches would be allowed to live a calm and peaceful life in secrecy, unbothered by the humans so long as we vowed to protect them from the vampires. However, putting all that pressure on our entire coven was a lot, so the Four decided to perform a spell that required they give up their lives and powers in order to create a *Chosen Protector*. This witch would be the most powerful witch of them all, sworn to defend the city from the darkest of evils. And there would always be One—as soon as she died, another would be called."

"But you haven't been living in secrecy. This entire town's *thing* is witches."

"Well, duh. They couldn't exactly erase history, so we just classified it under a mass murder which originated due to hysteria, Puritanical beliefs, and crazy paranoia. No one *actually* believes they were real witches. People just come here because they *want* to believe, even though they don't. It's a good time."

I choose then to pause and let James absorb some of what I've just told him.

"That was... a lot of information," he finally says.

I nod.

"So you were just chosen out of a group of girls to be this kick-ass vampire hunter?"

"I mean, kinda? The Magicks chose me, so I'm not sure how they would've been able to pass those powers onto someone else without my death. It's complicated, because the whole thing is supposed to be this great honor, but I hesitated to accept the role."

"What would've happened if you'd refused?"

I shrug, unsure. "I don't know. They kind of made it sound like I didn't have a choice at first, to be honest. But I was prepared to run off to Asia with you. Though they probably would've come after us."

James smiles, his eyes softening. "I would've run forever with you if we had to."

I can't help the goofy smile on my face. "And I would've loved every second of it."

He reaches out to take my hand and places a kiss on the back of it, his eyes closing as he inhales the scent of my skin. When he lowers my hand, his fingers twine with mine, and he never lets go.

Not until the doorbell rings, at least, with our dinner.

"It's your turn now," I say as I pull out our food from the delivery bag (two double bacon cheeseburgers and a large Coke for him—he was *ravenous*, he said—and a regular cheeseburger and Diet Coke for me). "Tell me what happened."

He exhales before unwrapping his burger, the smell of the beef and cheese filling my small loft. "I'm not sure, to be honest. Like I said, the last thing I remember is the fight that broke out after telling you I loved you. *Love* you." He shoots me a grin, and I can't help mine.

My heart does cartwheels in my chest, but I'm terrified. For the past year, it's been my job to fight off monsters and demons every day—but no fight or interaction with them has been as terrifying as this moment right now. What if it all goes away? What if it isn't even happening?

"After that, I have vague memories of being knocked

unconscious. Next thing I know, I'm waking up in this musty, damp room. No windows, no exit. No bathroom. They'd feed me every so often, but it was always under the door. I never so much as spoke or saw anyone until tonight, when those three vampires pulled me from my cell and told me I had somewhere to be. Then, right before you caught us, one of them said something like 'We should do it here.' Next thing I know, I'm being knocked on my ass by the edge of the trees. That's when one of them bit my throat. It was so fucking painful, Cate. I tried to fight them off and, as you can see, got beaten to a pulp." I wince when he points to his busted lip, his slightly bruised eye.

James's face *does* look like it's been through a fight, but it doesn't look as bad anymore.

Huh. The Healing potion works fast, but not *that* fast.

"After that, they kept trying to feed me something. It was so weird. A red liquid from a vial one of them pulled from their pocket, and—"

A metaphorical record scratch sounds over his voice.

"I'm sorry, what? They *fed* you something?" My heart takes off faster than I've ever felt it, the adrenaline speeding through my veins at an impossible speed. It's like my body knows what he's going to confirm before my brain does and is making sure I have the strength and will to accept it. To endure it.

James's nose scrunches in the most adorable way. "Yeah. And honestly? It tasted a little like blood."

And there's the other shoe dropping, I think. It lands like a damn anvil from the top of the Grand Canyon on my head,

Wile E. Coyote style. For a second there, I very nearly pass out.

As soon as I can speak, I get to my feet, jelly-legged, and walk over to my loft window. The moon is high in the sky, the city is quiet, and no one knows just how badly I want to cry right now. To scream in frustration.

"Did you drink it?" I ask him, my eyes on my reflection in the window. I should win an Oscar for how calm I'm able to act, considering. "The blood, I mean?"

Mid-bite, James responds with a muffled "They forced it down my throat. Kinda had to."

I suck in a breath and hold it in, feeling my lungs expand with every second that goes by. It won't be long now before he changes. It happens over a period of twenty-four hours. Or at least that's what The Society told me during training.

Almost in a trance, I wonder at what point in the transformation he will lose his soul. Wonder how much longer I have with my love before he's not only gone, but I have to end his life hours after finding our way back to each other.

"Cate?" James says my name like it isn't the first time he's called me. "Cate, baby. What's wrong?"

"How are you feeling?" I ask, finally turning to look at him. To *really* look at him. I do my best to absorb every single detail of the man in front of me. To remember these last few moments together. The slightly overgrown haircut and beard, only natural after a year of isolation. The same sparkling blue eyes where I imagined myself swimming so many times. His broad shoulders, which I so yearned to run my hands over. Feel the strength of his body and heart beneath my fingertips.

And now I won't have that.

"I—I told you. Good. Surprisingly not as sore as I thought I would be," he says with a rueful laugh. "To be honest, I'm not in as much pain anymore. I think—Whoa, hey. Why are you crying?"

I didn't even realize that I was. But then, a sob.

"James. I think you're a vampire."

CHAPTER SEVEN

James bursts out laughing. "What? I think I would know if I were a vampire, Cate."

Devastated, I say, "Maybe you aren't one now, but you're in transition. I think that's why you're still able to eat human food and... Well, anyway, soon enough you'll lose your soul, grow fangs, and only care for two things: human blood and the destruction of witches. You'll be evil. Dangerous. And then..."

I can't hold back my tears—they stream freely down my cheeks, my heart shattered into a million pieces almost making me wish he'd never come back. Especially since it's my responsibility to rid this town of vampires, and now that will include him.

James takes a deep breath and wipes his hands on a napkin before walking over to me. When he reaches my side, he cups my face with his right and holds my hip tightly with his left—staking a claim, while trying to comfort me. And I want that. I want him to stake a claim. I want him to hold me, to love me. I need him to tell me everything will be alright because I'm not sure I'll survive his death a second time. Not when it will be at my hands this time around.

"We don't even know whether I'm truly changing into a vampire. Maybe it was something else. Maybe they gave me a weird potion like you did, or—"

"James, c'mon." Sobbing, I let my forehead drop on his shoulder and wrap my arms around his waist.

He rubs his hands up and down my back in soothing motions.

It's heaven and hell.

"Cate, I love you," he whispers in my ear. "So much. I've loved you for over ten years—in the most consuming, deliciously torturous way. Since the very moment I laid eyes on you, I knew I was a goner. I have loved you, Cate, in a way that feels impossible for anyone else to know that kind of love. So I don't think anything will ever change that. Even if I do become a vampire, I could never lose my soul, Cate. Because you've owned it since the very second you said 'hello,' and I know you'd never let anything happen to it." James pulls away and tips my face back to look me in the eye before he continues: "But if I do lose it... If you *do* need to kill me. I forgive you. In fact—" He pauses to take a deep breath. "In fact, I give you *permission* to kill me. If I'm a danger to you and the rest of the world, then... then you should stop me."

"Don't say that," I mumble, pressing my face into his chest as I struggle to breathe through the crying. "Don't."

He sighs but doesn't argue.

After a minute, he pulls us down to my couch and holds me for several minutes as the exhaustion of the last few hours catches up with me.

"You're handling this all a bit too well," I whisper. "How

are you not freaking out? I mean, you were held captive for over a year. You haven't spoken to anyone in just as long. And now you might be a vampire and you're... just okay with it?"

He sighs. "Obviously not. I'm not okay, and I know there are many things I'm going to have to deal with. But right now, I just want to enjoy this time together. Especially if it's limited. I've been dreaming about reuniting with you every second of every day, so I'm not going to blow this opportunity on a mental breakdown."

I nod and exhale, inhaling the scent of him. It's not quite what I remember—a year of captivity will do that to someone—but it's still there beneath the musty smell of wherever the hell her was kept alive.

"Your food is getting cold," I whisper once I've settled a bit.

James laughs once. "I don't give a fuck. Even if it's congealed, it'll still be the best thing I've had in over a year. And this—being here for you and us—is more important than anything."

I fist my hands in his shirt—the same one he was wearing the last time I saw him. And it's right then that I realize something: "You probably haven't had a bath in a *looong* time." I pull away to meet his red face.

"I... no. I'm sorry if I stink and—" James begins to push me away, but I hold on.

"No, don't. I don't mind. Didn't even notice it, actually. I'm so happy to see you that—" I shake my head. "What I'm saying is... Do you want to shower? I can do your laundry, too. So you can change into clean clothes."

He laughs at my change in subject. "Really?"

"Really."

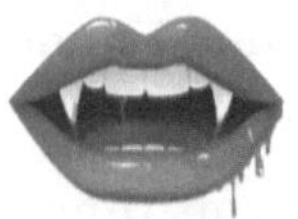

James spends over half an hour in the bathroom, and I don't blame him. If I were him and I'd spent the last year without so much as a sink, I'd be in there for over a full day (we all know my love of baths).

I'm thankful for the respite, for the opportunity to think about what comes next—even if I'm still drawing a blank—but part of me wished he'd said no to it. Part of me wished he'd said he wanted to spend every second we had together before it all comes to an end. Part of me wished he'd—

But then all of that regret disappears in an instant when he walks out of my bathroom in a cloud of steam like a fucking dream, droplets of water over his muscular chest, a towel that's way too small for him struggling to stay wrapped around his hips, the beginning of his v-line cut peeking out like a goddamn Adonis.

I could lick him dry.

"I... Your clothes aren't ready yet," I say, my voice sounding like it's miles away.

"That's okay." He grins.

And because I'm an idiot, all I can think to say is "Did you keep up a workout routine while you were in captivity or something?"

He sputters a laugh. "*What?*"

I shake my head, wanting to die. "Nothing."

James looks down at himself, seemingly realizing for the first time that he's basically naked. "Oh, you mean this?"

And then *drops.*

His.

Towel.

I stop breathing, because it's too much. I cannot multitask—between inhaling and focusing on the Greek god in front of me, I choose the latter. After all, how much longer of this will I have? My time with James is more finite than oxygen.

So I take a step forward and tentatively lift a hand, holding it just over his skin. Still hot from his shower, I can feel the heat radiate off him. Soon enough, once he's completed his transition, his body temperature will run low —a chilling fifty-ish degrees—but for now, the fire between us is scorching.

"You can touch me if you want," he says, his voice gravelly. Rough. Hungry.

Finally, I inhale a sharp breath. "I'm almost too scared to," I confess.

James takes my wrist and presses the palm of my hand right over his heart. It's still beating, though slower than it should be for your average adult male. So I focus on the drum, memorizing the beat. Tattooing it on the side of my brain to carry with me in the quiet times to come.

With incredible tenderness, he takes my other hand and places it right next to the first.

"Touch me," he almost groans.

With a sharp intake of breath, I follow orders. I've been such a good girl, too. I deserve this.

A rush of heat pools between my legs, my chest so tight there's not an ounce of air that would fit in my lungs right now. As I begin to move my hands over him, to feel the hard muscles of his shoulders and biceps, I can't help but admire the smoothness of his skin, the perfectly delicious way in which he looks down at me with a smirk that turns my legs to Jell-O and builds low in my stomach.

"Go lower," he murmurs.

I swallow, but there's a big lump in my throat making the task impossible. "I—Are you sure?" My voice is barely a squeak.

His smile is gentle when he nods, but the fire in his eyes is blazing.

With his permission, I venture down, running my fingers in between the lines of his abdomen, admiring every dip and hill, the light smattering of hair—his happy trail—leading all the way down to where I can feel he's already hard. I bring both hands down the sides of his ribs and admire how they taper into his waist and hips. And that's where I stop to *really* look. To gawk, really. To drag the tips of my fingers down that delicious V. Down those defined muscles that lead directly to his cock.

A cock that has me gasping in shock, burning at the cheeks, and aching in between my legs.

"*James*," I moan, unable to take my eyes off him. *It.*

"Yeah?"

I nod.

"Can I...?"

"*God*, yes. Please," he begs.

It's only then that I notice his panting, the look of desperation in his eyes. And it makes me feel all-powerful and invincible—more than winning any fight with vampires ever has. Because this perfect, gorgeous, sweet, intelligent man wants me. Wants *me*. How is that even possible?

My gaze lifts to meet his just before I wrap my hand around his cock—hard, thick, warm, and perfect. And the way his eyes roll to the back of his head is everything—the validation I need to know that I'm not the only one about to spontaneously combust from this encounter.

"Harder," he says with a groan. "I like it *rough*." His confession burns my cheeks, heats my skin.

He gasps. "Your hand. It just got hot."

I pull it away, embarrassed beyond belief. "I'm so sorry. Sometimes, when I'm very emotional, my powers... They just—"

"You lose control?"

I sigh. "Yeah. I'm sorry."

Something in his expression shifts. Like he's... proud of himself for it?

"Don't apologize." And with speed that rivals my own movements in battle, he pulls my face to his, wraps an arm around my waist, and kisses me as if we were an inch from death.

And aren't we, though?

But I couldn't care less. You couldn't pay me to care about anything other than this moment right here, right now, in James's arms as he paws at my clothes. Pulls at my pants and manages to push them down without ever even unbuttoning them. Lifts the hem of my henley and pulls it over my head.

Before I even realize it, I'm fully naked—where did my underwear go?—swept up in James's arms, and thrown on my bed.

CHAPTER EIGHT

"We probably shouldn't be doing this. You know, considering," I manage to whisper—and hate myself for it immediately after.

Luckily, James is the voice of *un*reason. "If I only have a few hours left before I lose myself, then… Well, then, I actually want to *lose* myself in you."

He crawls over me, kissing up my abdomen, in between my breasts as he does. That's where he stops. Where he licks and sucks. Where he moves to one of my nipples and traces it with his tongue while his fingers pinch the other.

I arch off the bed, crying out his name. There's a warm, heavy feeling in between my legs, wetness pooling faster than it ever has for anyone—even for the James I often fantasized about.

No one has ever wanted anyone more than I want him.

"You're so soft," he breathes against my skin before taking my nipple between his teeth. He tugs gently, but just enough that I feel it all the way between my legs. My pussy clenches around nothing, aching from feeling so empty. "I've dreamt about running my tongue over this perfect skin for so long, and now that I can..." He shivers. "Cate, this is so much better than I ever could've imagined."

I groan and nod, a bit desperate—but too far gone to care how I sound.

"What do you need? Tell me what you need." His voice shares the same urgency I feel.

I reach down to grab his shoulders, reach up to cup his face. "You. I just need you. Before this is all gone and taken away from us."

James swallows once before nodding and moving up my body. I feel his hard cock—heavy, smooth, warm—press against my folds when he settles between my thighs.

"*Jesus*, you're so fucking wet."

My hand wraps around him, feeling the perfect weight of him. With care, I drag the tip of his penis over my wetness, letting him feel how crazy he makes me. How out of control.

His head drops between his shoulders with a groan. With his forehead pressed against my neck, he groans out my name.

"I don't think I can wait much longer," I tell him.

"Then let's not."

Without another word, one of his hands drags down my side, over my ribs and waist, down my thigh. He stops at my knee and hooks it over his hip with the confidence and command of someone who knows what to do with my body, even though we've never done this before.

It's a tight fit, but after a few gentle thrusts, he manages to push all the way in. That's where the delicateness ends, though. Because as soon as he's seated all the way inside me, I gasp, cry out his name, and he loses it.

James's thrusts are rough and demanding—not fast or hurried, but *thorough*. Enthusiastic. Like he's here to get the job done, yes, but he's here to do it *well*. Better than anyone else.

He scoops me off the mattress, arms ensnaring my waist, as his hips piston into me with a force that leaves me gasping for breath, on the verge of death, yet begging for more.

He's so big, the stretch is a bit painful and a lot delicious. I never want it to end.

His body surrounds me—his heat, the sound of his filthy voice in my ear (*...so fucking wet...so good...want you dripping in my come...*), his bergamot scent—and it's all I've ever wanted. All I'll ever want.

It's beautiful and devastating at the same time, because I know in that moment that, once he's gone, I will never be happy again. Not after this.

As I near my orgasm—barrel towards it, more like—something around us changes. The dim lighting in the room evolves into bright lights, originating from somewhere unknown. When I finally come, it hits me in waves, and the entire room bursts in flashes and sparks, immersing us in stardust.

I barely notice, though. And neither does James, since I feel every muscle in his body tense. The movements in his hips grow impossibly rougher and off-rhythm, though still euphoric. And when I realize he's just seconds away from his release, I wrap my arms around him and dig my nails into his back, begging him to come inside.

And that's his last straw. The last bit of restraint disappears. With his loss of control comes another orgasm for me.

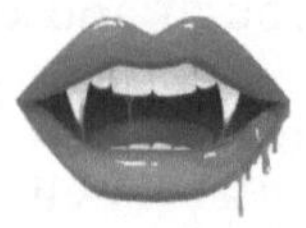

James pushes a strand of hair off my face, a soft, goofy smile spreading across his. "That was incredible."

We're both on our sides, naked in bed, enjoying every second of this post-coital bliss as the sun begins to rise.

"It was." I lean forward to press a soft kiss on his lips, but it soon grows. Evolves into a deep-rooted hunger that seems to never go away. "It *is*," I say, pushing him on his back as I straddle him.

"Fuck, yeah," he groans when I settle over his cock, rocking over him so he can feel my puffy lips—still wet from our combined come.

I fold over him to kiss his up his perfect chest all the way to his neck. It's there that I pause, my entire blood running cold.

"Your vampire bite."

His smirk falls. "Do we need to talk about this *now*? What about it?"

"It's gone."

James sits up beneath me and wraps his arms around my waist. When he looks up at me, his voice is full of tenderness. Of calm strength. "Baby, it could've just been your Healing potion. Remember?"

"The Healing Potion takes longer to work. You're not just back to 100% a few hours after drinking it. And your bruises..." I run my fingers over his cheekbone. The black eye that had started to form is long-gone, replaced only by redness. His busted lip is healed, too.

"I'm telling you, I feel totally normal. I think they never intended for me to turn into a vampire. I think if they did, we dodged a bullet, because I feel great." He grins, trying to lighten the mood.

And at first it works—but only for a few seconds. Because as I stare at his beautiful smile, I notice a hint of two sharp teeth peeking out from beneath James's lips.

Fangs.

"Shit."

Just then, my phone rings on my bedside table. Ian's name flashes.

"I don't know what to do. What to say."

"To me or to him?" James asks when I jump off him.

Scrambling for some clothes in my closet, my heart races, fear overtaking my system. My phone keeps ringing, but I refuse to pick it up. Lying to The Society seems unnatural, but betraying James is unthinkable.

As I begin to pull on a fresh pair of underwear, I wonder: am I going to dress for a fight or for comfort? Is he five seconds from turning on me? Or has he done so already and is pretending like everything is fine so he can get me to lower my guard and murder me? At what point in the transition do vamps lose their souls? I don't think I was ever taught that in witch lessons.

Because I have no idea what to tell him, I decide it's best not to try and fill the silence.

"Can you talk to me? Can you please tell me what's going

on?" His voice is so inherently *James*, though, that I can't help breaking my rule.

"I just... I need to prepare myself."

His expression is quizzical at first, until the other shoe drops. "Oh. To kill me, you mean."

I nod, choking up.

"I see." James exhales, resigned, before feeling his fangs with the tips of his fingers. "They're pretty sharp," he says with awe.

This makes me sputter a laugh.

"What?"

"Just..." I shrug. "I don't know. I love you."

His answering smile is sad. "I know. I'm sorry you have to go through this."

I sniff and wipe my nose with the back of my hand. "You feel sorry for me for having to kill you?"

"Of course." He frowns, like his reasoning is obvious. "Why is it hard to believe?"

"Because you're the one who has to die." The sharp pain in my chest as I speak the words aloud is nearly debilitating.

"I know, baby. But I'm not the one who is going to have to live with it."

Something slices right through my heart, cutting it in half.

As I bleed out, I sigh and finish dressing—for comfort, because I'm not ready to end the love of my life. Not today.

"The Society is looking for me. I didn't check in after going out hunting last night, which I usually do. You know, to make sure I didn't die and they don't have to call upon another."

"So why don't you just answer the phone? Just tell them you're alive."

I sit beside James and slump against his shoulder. "Because there was obviously some foul play surrounding your death. Or fake death. And I don't think I'd be able to stop myself from asking them point-blank what happened. I don't know who I can trust. Don't know who I should talk to. Something isn't right here, and I need to do more research before I tell absolutely anyone about you."

His arm comes around me. It feels like coming home for the first time. James kisses the top of my head before pulling away to look me straight in the eye.

"How can I help?" he asks, his gaze filled with so much love and support I nearly throw myself at him once again.

Smiling, I get to my feet. "Not sure whether you can do anything, to be honest. Any second now you'll... Well, and anyway, contrary to what movies show you, I doubt turning into a vampire automatically makes you a black belt in taekwondo. If we were to encounter some bad people, I'd be distracted the entire time making sure you'd be fine. It's best if you stay here, out of sight."

"Yeah, but I'm basically immortal, though, right? So what does it matter? I won't get hurt."

"I mean, sure, you're *basically* immortal. You heal fast and you're much stronger than you were as a human, but you still have vulnerabilities. Can't go out in the sun. Stake through the heart. You know, the usual."

James laughs. "The usual? Baby, none of this is the usual. Not witches, not vampires, not us."

I frown. "What do you mean 'not us'?"

He smiles and walks over to me—buck naked—before cupping my face and placing a soft kiss on my lips. "I meant that we—what we have—is one of a kind. I can't imagine anyone else feeling this way. I don't think it's possible for anyone to care for you the way I do."

My answering kiss is more like a goofy smile pressed against his lips. He's so fucking adorable.

CHAPTER
NINE

I'm not usually someone who makes stupid choices—
and I really hope today is not an exception.

After our conversation, I decide that leaving James
alone in my apartment with all my weapons and potions
seems like a marvelously idiotic idea, so I decide to bring him
with me—hidden beneath a very strong Invisibility spell and
a tricky, yet effective Linking spell that stops James from
getting more than six feet away from me. You know, just in
case he flips his switch and tries to make a run for it. Addi-
tionally, in order to protect him from the sunlight, I cast an
Engulfing spell that will keep him from bursting into flames.

Magic is useful like that.

It's still dangerous to bring him along, but what else was
I supposed to do? I mean, I couldn't just leave him alone, and
I had research to do. And there was no way I was going to tell
The Society he was still alive, so I couldn't leave him with
them. *Definitely* wasn't going to tell them about the whole
vampire thing. At least not until I find the person responsible
for infiltrating our team and faking James's death. Clearly,
this is a collaboration between the vampires and one or more
of the witches, and something about *certain people's* general

shitty attitude and his post as a pathologist tells me I already know who it is. So after checking in with The Society and providing proof of life, I head over to the city morgue.

It doesn't take much to convince the front desk and security guards to let me through. All I need is a Compelling spell to get them to agree and hand me the keys and a Memory spell so they forget I was even there.

In the main computer, James and I quickly find his autopsy report. In it, it's clearly stated that James's cause of death was due to an animal attack—pretty standard when hiding a vampire-related death. However, even in the rush to falsify reports, there are no fake pictures, no made-up descriptions of injuries like there usually would be. Nothing. The whole thing is basically blank.

Of course, since they didn't find a body, it's logical. James was never *really* dead, was he?

Now he is, I think glumly. I shake my head and try not to dwell on that for the moment.

But still, shouldn't they be putting in a little more effort? Doctor some pictures or something? It's just the sloppiness that surprises me. This isn't our regular MO.

When I check for the name of the examining pathologist, I find the exact thing I need to confirm my suspicions:

```
Patient: Kittle, James
Age: 28 years old
Cause of Death: animal attack
Chief Pathologist/Examiner: Dr. Ian
McCaffrey
Notes: N/A
```

There it is.

Ian's the one who signed off on this farce.

"Holy shit," James whispers when I show him the file. "That motherfucker seriously signed off on this. Your own Handler fucking betrayed you and your entire operation."

I swallow and nod. "Ian and I have always butted heads, but this is..."

With the ire and fire of a thousand suns, I pull my phone out of my pocket, take pictures of the report, and message The Society requesting an emergency meeting without giving many details as to why.

I anxiously pace around The Society's headquarters—an old Victorian home that looks practically condemned on the outside but has everything needed to manage a tactical operation and probably even an apocalyptic event, CCTV of the entire town, weaponry, ingredients for any type of potion you can dream of, and an underground library so large it rivals the Library of Congress—all while wondering how the hell I was going to break the news to everyone that we had a traitor in our midst. A traitor who, for some inexplicable reason, has been working with the vampires. I don't know why the hell Ian did what he did, but I know he double-crossed us, and it's vital we figure out why and put an end to it.

A restrained James stands beside me as we whisper to

each other what the plan should be. No one who passes by can see or hear him but me, so I look psychotic, but that's fine.

"Catie." Matilda, my friend and one of the members of The Society's Council, interrupts our conversation. "What's going on? What's the emergency?"

James tenses beside me, but I'm so relieved to see a friendly face that I sigh.

Matilda and I used to be very close—though not as close as James and I have been. During our early childhood years Matilda and I spent almost every second together, especially since our moms used to be best friends. When my mother killed herself after my dad left and I had to move into my aunt's house, Matilda came over to check on me every day. Unfortunately, we've grown apart since college, but there has never been any bad blood between us. There isn't a doubt in my mind this woman had nothing to do with any of this.

"I think it's best to tell everyone at once, Tilly," I say, glad for her arrival. It gives me the final confidence to walk into the main office where I spot the leaders of the council seated around the round table.

Tilly walks over as head representative of her family beside my aunt Cybil, who, as Keeper of our History, was probably already in the office to begin with. It's where she volunteers on days the shop is closed.

As Handler of the Chosen Protector, Ian is seated at the head of the table. I take my assigned spot at the other end while James stands beside me, undetected.

Bringing in a vampire into our headquarters is madness, it's true. I'm just glad no one else can see him but me.

"This is highly irregular of you to call for an emergency meeting, Hecate. I'm surprised you didn't come to me first before triggering our emergency comms policy. You know these protocols are reserved for *real* emergencies, correct? Not one of your silly dramas."

I suppress the urge to roll my eyes at him and instead settle for smiling tightly in his direction. After, I greet all twelve members, calling each one by their first and last names, doing my best to show them some kind of respect and admiration.

To be honest, if there were a "Most Respectful and Obedient Protector Award" I would not be the one winning it. I am the first to admit that over the past year, I've been surly and despondent. Definitely a tad rebellious. A particularly gigantic pain in The Society's ass. However, because I've done a fantastic job at fighting vampires and keeping the supernatural order in Salem, The Society hasn't given me *as much* shit as I deserve.

Still, it makes me nervous for what I'm about to say. Because what if they don't believe me? What if it's a miss, and this whole thing gets turned around on me? After all, I'm the one harboring a fucking vampire. I'm the one *literally* sleeping with the enemy—though they definitely don't need to know about the multiple orgasms James just spent the last twelve hours giving me (who knew vamp sex was so fucking hot, anyway?).

"This isn't a *silly drama*. And I don't think bringing this concern directly to you would've been a good idea—especially when it's in regard to your traitorous behavior."

There's a collective gasp around the table, and if I weren't so nervous, I'd almost laugh.

Ian narrows his eyes at me. "What the hell are you talking about?"

"I'm talking about you working with the vampires. About you creating some sort of fucked up alliance and lying to this entire council."

Rex Shepherd, one of the oldest members of the council, speaks up first. "What's the meaning of this, McCaffrey? What is she talking about?"

Ian scoffs. "I don't know what she means. I have dedicated my entire life to The Society and its cause—unlike Miss Goode, here, who didn't even want to accept the Protector role to begin with."

Now I allow myself to roll my eyes at him. "*As if.* Sorry for having *one* goddamn moment of hesitation while I decided whether or not to take a fucking life-changing responsibility on. But that was a year ago, and you and I both know that as soon as the Initiation ceremony was complete, I have been nothing but dedicated to my role as Protector."

"I wouldn't have hesitated for a single *second*. In fact, no one at this goddamn table would've thought about it twice." He grits his teeth like he's holding so much more back.

"I find it *a bit* hard to believe that in the past three hundred plus years, not a single Protector candidate has ever thought, 'Oh, hey, maybe I *don't* want to spend the rest of my life fighting vampires and giving up my future in order to keep the city safe. Maybe I want to think of my own happiness.'"

Out of the corner of my eye, I watch Cybil's face drop in her hands, while some of the older members shift uncomfortably in their seats. The younger members and I, on the other hand, remain a bit lost.

Ian's eyes brighten with an evil smirk on his face, as if to say, *'I've got you now, kid.'*

"Oh, there was definitely one other person who thought of rejecting the role. But she crumbled under the pressure of it all before she could even formally decline. See, the Goode family is made up of weak blood," he sneers.

Cybil's head snaps up and glares at Ian. "You shut your mouth before speaking another word against us."

He laughs darkly. "Fine. I won't say much more except for this: you know I respect *you*, Cybil, but your family is a disgrace. The Magicks selected *two* Chosen Protectors from the same bloodline—who the hell knows why—and both have ended up being massive disappointments."

My stomach sinks. They can't really be talking about... "What are you talking about? What do you mean?"

"Your mother. You didn't know she was selected as Chosen Protector when you were just a child?"

"*What?*" I gasp.

I feel more than see the way James tenses beside me. His hands rest over my shoulders in a feeble attempt to calm me down.

"You never thought to tell me about this, Cybil?"

My aunt pulls her brows together, disgust on her face. "Why would I?"

"Uh, I don't fucking know. Maybe because *I'm* the freaking Protector now? You don't think it was relevant?" My voice drips with sarcasm and disdain. "Maybe because I've been begging for scraps of information about my mother for two decades, and you refuse to give me anything but crumbs? Maybe I would've felt a bit more understood and less alone knowing that she went through the same thing. Had the same doubts?"

"She was a disappointment." Cybil rolls her eyes.

"You cannot be serious. She was sick! She had a mental illness!" Someone *must* have possessed my aunt or something, because she would never speak ill of my mother. Never has in all these years.

"This... seems like a personal conversation," Tilly breathes, pushing away from her seat as she gazes nervously at the council members sitting around the table. Each one looks more uncomfortable than the next.

"Sit down," I command.

"Right." She settles back in her seat, and so does everyone else.

"We haven't even gotten to why I've brought us all here."

"Fine, then. Get it over with," Ian says, crossing his arms in front of his chest.

I sigh and take a deep breath. I'll deal with my aunt later. "Okay. Well. I'm here to accuse Dr. Ian McCaffrey of working with the vampires in order to sabotage this council, The Society, and my life. I accuse him of faking the death of James Kittle, and of aiding and abetting his kidnapping. I accuse him of using magic and influence to corrupt our governmental system."

"You're incredible," James whispers in my ear. I smile triumphantly, readying myself for my big win.

Except—

"Are you insane?" Ian's voice booms. "How *dare* you accuse me of all these crimes? What kind of evidence do you even have? And why are you bringing up anything related to James when he's been dead for over a year?"

"Because he's not," Cybil's voice—small, yet strong—sneaks up on us.

CHAPTER TEN

I can't help my gasp as I stare, wide-eyed, at the woman who raised me. "Aunt Cybbie? How do *you* know that?"

"Wait, hold on." Ian glances back and forth between us. "What's going on?"

"You mean you don't know?" I ask him.

"Know what?"

With the wave of her hand, Tilly forces all the doors of the meeting room closed, locking them with a spell. The sound of the locks clicking into place reverberates through the room, echoing off the mahogany walls, each *click* sending shivers down my spine.

"Okay, then," she says, her voice taking on one of authority. "Someone better start talking. Fast."

The rest of the council nods, each one with a stern expression on their face.

Heart racing, I glance anxiously between my aunt and Ian, epically confused. "Well, I thought... Aunt Cybil?"

My aunt sighs and rolls her eyes at me. "You really are just as idiotic as your mother, aren't you? Just as ungrateful, too."

"I—" I genuinely don't know what to say.

"Cybil, this is *highly* irregular," Jane Winthropp, an old friend of my mother's, speaks up.

"Oh, *shut up*, Janie. You and I both know Isobel was a waste of a Protector. We complained enough about it all the time when she was first selected."

"Still, it isn't right to speak ill of the dead."

"Really?" Cybil raises an accusatory brow. "Then why is it that I've had to deal with the constant whispers of this entire group since the death of my sister? Why is it that my family isn't allowed to move on from it?"

"I—" Jane stutters, but drops her eyes to her neatly folded hands in her lap.

"I don't understand," I say. "What does any of this have to do with—"

"Ugh!" Cybil bangs her fists on the table and gets to her feet. "Are you an idiot? I thought I raised you better than that. *I* was the one who organized James's abduction with the vampires."

"*What?*" I screech. "But James's autopsy shows it was Ian who—"

"Well, I obviously wasn't going to write my name, was I? So I used his. Used a bit of olde magic to get Ian to give me all his passwords and such."

The entire Council is outraged, screaming at Cybil and me and everyone around us.

"You—*What?*" Ian gasps.

Meanwhile, I'm on the verge of losing control. And more importantly, I don't care. My skin is a destructive wildfire, so much so that the chair beneath me begins to smoke, its fabric slowly burning.

"Baby, you need to stop," James speaks beside me. "You're going to spontaneously combust or something."

"I *can't*," I murmur, seeing literal red. Because I am about to *end* her.

"Take a breath, Cate. Take a breath and try to focus."

But I steadily ignore him. Instead, I choose to get to my feet.

Cybil glares at me. "Don't you dare, you little twit."

Her words are like a slap across the face. The kind of punch in the gut that knocks the air out of you and leaves you immobilized.

The anger and resentment I feel emanating from my aunt surprises me. In my 29 years of life, I have never felt anything but support from her, and now this?

The fire spreading across my body doesn't fade, so much as evolve into ice. Every inch of me goes cold.

"Cate," James whispers again, even though no one can hear him—especially not through all the arguing and yelling. The rest of the Council members are not happy with Cybil, and they're making it very known. "Cate you need to release me from the restraints. She has *that look* in her eyes. The kind bad people get before they're about to do bad things."

My first instinct is to tell him he's overreacting. After all, why would my aunt want to harm me? But then I remember *she fucking tried to ruin my life* and figure he may have a point.

Except... what if this is the moment he loses his soul? What if it disappears when he's freed from all that makes him good and it's my fault I let an invisible vampire into our headquarters to murder all the members of our council?

James senses my hesitation. "Baby, I promise. If I turn

into some evil monster, kill me, okay? But I have a feeling something bad is going to happen."

I nod and snap my fingers, releasing him from any restraints or links. For obvious reasons, I keep him invisible.

"THAT'S IT!" Cybil screams over the arguing, bringing me back to the moment. "I've had it with all of you." With a swipe of her hands and an incantation I've never heard of before, in a language I don't recognize, she ties every member of the Council, including myself, to their chair with ropes that appear out of thin air. With a second motion, she slaps a Silencing spell on everyone else but me.

"What the hell are you doing?" My world has been turned upside down, and I'm completely lost. These past twenty-four hours have been an absolute roller coaster I definitely want to get off.

"*Fuck*," James says. "I'm going to take her down. When the moment is right, I'll take her down."

"I need to hear what you did, Cybil," I say, for his benefit and hers. I need him to know to stand down. At least until I hear everything she has to say.

James shoots me a quiet nod and goes to stand by Cybil, ready to take her on when she least expects it.

"I am *tired* of this family's reputation being tarnished by the selfish behaviors of its members! First your mother, and now you. It wasn't enough to have your mother reject the post of Protector simply because your pathetic father couldn't accept she was a witch. No, you had to follow in her footsteps and do the absolute same thing!"

Tears stream down my cheeks, warming my cool skin. Hearing the woman who raised me say that *she* was the traitor has left a hole inside my stomach. "What did you do?" I rasp.

She shrugs, nonchalant. "I reached out to one of the leaders of a vampire clan and offered him protection so long as he helped me get rid of James. You were too wrapped up in your *childish* crush," she spits out, disgusted. "This family couldn't afford another member rejecting this most sacred position. I mean, why the Magicks picked you two instead of *me*, someone who is utterly devoted to this cause, is insanity! So I wanted James dead. I wanted this strong connection to your non-witch life gone—and he was supposed to be. It wasn't until early this morning that I got a message from one of the vampires of the clan I worked with saying James had escaped."

Cybil scoffs before continuing, flipping her auburn hair over her shoulder. "I cannot express my rage. He was supposed to be dead! 'Mangled beyond recognition,' is what they told me. You don't need to worry about them, my dear Hecate. I've taken care of them. No one betrays me and gets away with it. But where is James now? So I can finish him off."

"You stay the hell away from him," I practically growl.

James takes another step toward Cybil, ready to pounce on my command. In the back of my mind, I admire the poise, strength, and self-control he has to overcome the urge to murder the person who is responsible for having him locked up for over a year. I would've ripped her throat out already. I want to.

Cybil laughs at my outrage. "Is he still human? Or did the vampires turn him? Either way, it doesn't matter. This will all be over in a minute, and then I'll find him and kill him myself."

"I cannot believe you. How could you do that? How could you just stand there and so openly admit to wanting to murder James? He was the love of my life. He was everything to me."

"Oh, please," she rolls her eyes at me. "I wanted his death to give you an insatiable hunger for revenge, and it worked. The final push to get you to accept your role. It turned you into a better-than-average Protector."

"I'm a fucking *amazing* Protector, you jealous, back-stabbing bitch."

James grins proudly in my direction, a crooked smile that would otherwise turn my legs to jelly.

Cybil narrows her green eyes at me, not impressed by my vocabulary. "Contrary to what you believe, Hecate, I didn't do anything new. The witches have secretly worked with the vampires—or used them—many, *many* times over the years."

"What the hell are you talking about?"

She laughs softly. "How else do you think we saved ourselves from the Salem Witch Trials?"

CHAPTER ELEVEN

I feel my brows pull together in confusion, my face the only part of my body not frozen by her spell.

"The Society and the vampires have worked together *several* times. The first was when we were getting murdered left and right by the disgusting humans. So The Four decided to get creative and bring a few vampires from the Old World. They promised them an open buffet if they started killing off the Puritans responsible for the Trials. But really, we just wanted a faux common enemy with the humans. Something to get them to need us."

"So we double-crossed the vampires?" I ask, shocked.

She nods, a sly grin spreading across her face.

"Are you serious?" My whole training has been a lie?

Cybil laughs. "The Four were truly brilliant for informing the vampires where most of the town would be the night of their trial. But then, once they arrived to terrorize the humans, our own Society betrayed them and sold them out to the humans, making us a necessary 'evil' in order to secure the town's safety.

"Obviously, the vampires who got away did not appreciate it, so we've been at odds ever since. But that doesn't mean that we haven't worked together again with the more free-agent vampires. Every time some ridiculous new political candidate starts to gain ground or anti-witch sentiment grows with the locals, we find ways to work together in lucrative deals."

"I..." Don't know what to say.

I look around the table at the more senior members of the Council and take in their guilt-ridden expressions, their mouths pressed shut by Cybil's obscure incantation. Disappointed by how messed up the internal workings of our organization are, I take comfort in one thing: regardless of whatever dark magic Cybil might be using right now, there's no way she can hold this spell for much longer. Not when she's using it on so many people at the same time. And she's definitely no match for me in a duel—I'm still the Chosen Protector, after all.

"What do you intend to do now, Cybil? Off the entire Council?" I scoff. "You'd never get away with it. The rest of the witches of Salem wouldn't let you."

She shrugs, relaxed. "Who knows? Maybe they're tired of this Protector BS. And maybe the new mayor might want to actually work with me once I show him I had to get rid of the Council after I found out about their corrupt dealings with the vampires. Maybe, for once, I'll get what I deserve."

"Oh, I think you'll get *exactly* what you deserve," I sneer. "James, *now!*"

Cybil's eyes widen in realization, her head turning quickly in every direction as she searches for my love. But it's only when he tackles her to the ground that she realizes he's under an Invisibility spell.

"How did you do it? How did you manage to hold a spell like that for so long?" She screams as James holds her down. "I was monitoring you through the town's CCTV since you left your apartment earlier this morning, and I never saw him."

Free from her magical shackles, I run over to Cybil and James's side. I remove the incantation, revealing a gorgeous James to the entire Council—all of whom have now been released as well.

"I told you," I say, golden ropes wrapping around her body like a boa constrictor, restraining her physically and magically. "I'm stronger. Better. Faster. *Smarter* than you could ever hope to be. And so was my mother. A Goode woman was destined to be the Protector, that's for sure. But it was never going to be you, Aunt Cybil. You could never measure up to my mother or myself."

With a final wave of my hand, I send another golden rope her way, this time serving as a gag.

CHAPTER TWELVE

"Let's go home?" I ask James as we watch The Society Guards take Cybil away, where she'll be locked up in the dungeons while she awaits trial.

His answering sad smile is disorienting.

"What?"

"You said 'home.' I haven't had that in a long time. Kinda sad I won't anymore."

"What do you mean?"

"You know... You're going to have to—" He runs his fingers across his throat, mock-slitting it.

"Well, I'd probably be driving a stake through your heart, to be honest. Or setting you on fire. Cutting your head off *is* an option, but it's super messy." I try for a smile, but it comes out mangled.

James reaches out to take my hand in his. "Can we just enjoy the last of what little time we have left?"

"*Please.*"

With a quick goodbye, Tilly promises to keep me updated on anything she finds out about what the Senior Council have been hiding.

"I know as the Protector I should stay, but..." I grimace.

"Go. We've got this handled," she promises. "And I'll text you when I find out more about the whole soul thing," she adds in a whisper so low I hope James's supernatural hearing can't pick it up. By the look on his face, however, it's clear he heard every word. "But honestly, with every second that goes by, I'm thinking it was all a hoax. Two corrupt groups working together to terrorize a town."

We sneak out back, avoiding the curious glances of the Council, the guards, and other members of the witch community who have shown up to help detangle the mess that has become our organization.

Once we're in my loft, it doesn't take long before James gently pushes me on the bed. Before he crawls over my body and presses the most perfect kiss to my lips—a combination of hunger and sweetness all wrapped in one—and wraps his arms around me.

"If we could have forever, would you take it?" he asks suddenly after a long moment of peaceful and comfortable silence.

"What do you mean?" I sit up to look him straight in the eye.

James sighs. "You know what I mean. If you could turn— if *I* could turn you... Would you want to?"

"I..." I think of an eternity of James. Of *this*. Of *us*.

'Joy' and 'elation' aren't strong enough words to describe the feeling that shoots through my veins—like glitter coursing through my blood, shining and humming in anticipation of a never-ending life beside my love.

"I want to say yes. In fact, I want to beg for you to do it."

"But?" His blue eyes stare deep into my soul, hesitant and patient.

"But I spent my whole life thinking vampires were evil, and the last year fighting them to the death. I gave up every part of myself so I could be as dedicated as possible to this cause. Which has led me into kinda the middle of an existential crisis now. If vampires don't lose their soul, then what does that mean for me as Protector? If I become a vampire, do I lose my witch powers? And if I don't, what does that make me?"

"I think we've proved that vampires can choose to be bad or good, because I'm still here. I'm still yours."

"Yes, you are," I breathe. *Thank the gods.*

"And that also means that there will always be bad vampires. Which means you'll still have business as a Protector."

"But what if we're mistaken? What if you're the exception, and I really do end up losing my soul?"

"Not possible," he says, shaking his head. "I won't let you. Just as you own mine, I own yours."

My answering smile is rueful.

"Listen, I'm not going to pressure you. But if it turns out that you don't have to kill me... I just want to be with you. Always. We've lost so much time, and—" He sighs and runs both his hands through his hair, eyes squeezed shut. When he finally seems to calm down, he continues: "I just want forever. I know it's selfish and fucked up, and I didn't even know the possibility existed until less than twenty-four hours ago, but I don't care. I want it. With you."

Eyes wet, I gently pull James's face into a kiss. With

everything I have, I pour all my love into it, hoping somehow he can feel how much I care about him. How much I want an eternity with him, as well.

"I—" I begin to say but am cut off by an incessant buzzing in my jeans' back pocket. "Sorry, let me—" When I go to turn it off, however, a message from Tilly cuts me off:

TILLY

Go for it, friend. It was all a lie. James has more soul than most of this Senior Council could ever hope to have combined.

I suck in a breath, suddenly on top of the world.

"What? What is it?"

With a grin that could rival the Cheshire Cat, I launch myself onto James, wrapping my arms around his neck as I plant a kiss on his lips.

He doesn't hesitate, choosing instead to go with the moment.

"I love you, James Kittle."

He sputters a laugh against my mouth. "I love you, too, Cate Goode."

"Will you take a bath with me?"

His crooked smile makes my heart thump so loudly in my ears, I barely hear him when he says, "Baby, I thought you'd never ask."

CHAPTER THIRTEEN

James reaches out to offer his hand for balance, so I take it as I step into the tub, feeling his rough palm against the smoothness of mine.

I love his hands. I love how they work. I love how he plays me like an instrument with them, making me come as easily as if he could read my mind. How he holds me with so much love and care and devotion, like he'll never let go. How he loves me with them in a way no one has ever been loved before.

James shoots me a smirk as I dip my feet in the hot water. It's like he knows what I'm thinking, like he can read every minuscule expression on my face. He spreads his legs as far apart as they can go and slowly helps me to sit between them. With care, I lean back against his warm chest once seated, feeling his hard cock press against my lower back as I rest my head against his shoulder. When his arms wrap tightly around me, I sigh happily.

I'm in heaven.

"You are the most incredible thing that has ever happened to me, Hecate Goode," he whispers in my ear before pressing a kiss to my neck.

"You're just saying that because I saved your life."

He play-growls. "Don't be self-effacing, love. I can't stand it. I don't love you because you saved my life, but just so you know, you didn't just save it last night. You saved it the second I met you. You saved me from loneliness. From being the sad, almost-orphan when I first got to college. You saved me from myself after my mother died and I became an actual orphan. We're different, but somehow cut from the same cloth, so you get me. Every day, you've been my savior, and that was way before you ever became the Chosen Protector." James tightens his arms around me.

I fight back tears and sniffle. "I love you."

He inhales the scent of my skin as if I were the most incredible drug. "I love you, too, Cate." A kiss on my jugular. Another on the ball of my shoulder. "You smell incredible, by the way. Better than I remember. And you're perfect. A goddess. You can't deny it. Especially not with those powers."

I frown, thankful he can't see the expression on my face. "So it's my powers you like?"

He scoffs. "I wasn't talking about your magic. I worshipped at your feet *before* I knew you were a witch. I was the sole member of The Church of Cate and thrilled about it. Less so when I thought you didn't return my feelings, but, my god," he says with a sigh, shaking his head in wonder. "Those short minutes we had together before everything went to shit were amazing. To be honest, it was the thought of seeing you again that kept me alive all that time I was imprisoned."

My heart wrenches in my chest, body tensing. He feels every inch of the shift in my body language.

"Baby, no," he whispers in my ear, pulling back my hair so he can reach more of my neck, place kisses on my wet skin from my jaw to the tip of my shoulder. "Don't. We're here now, aren't we?"

"Are we? I can't be sure. I still don't know whether this is a dream or reality. I've fantasized about this very moment more times than I can count. In this tub, too."

He chuckles, the mood quickly shifting back into something lighter. "Oh, yeah? Like what?"

I twist in his arms and lightly slap him on the shoulder. "C'mon."

"I'm serious. You gonna tell me about them or what?"

"Mmm." I lean back against his chest again, wrap his arms loosely around my waist. Tracing the tattoo he got his sophomore year on his inner forearm, I admire the cords of his muscles. Feel the heat of him beneath my fingertips. Dream of those arms holding my hands above my head as he enters me. Suddenly, my skin flushes a deep crimson.

He notices with a chuckle.

One of James's hands begins a titillating trajectory down my chest, between my breasts. He stops for a moment to circle one of my nipples—to pinch and tug it while I moan in pleasure. Heat that has nothing to do with the hot water starts to build between my legs, a delicious empty feeling building low in my stomach.

"Cate," he whispers in my ear, his voice taking a dark tone. "If you tell me about your fantasies, I may just make them come true, baby."

I whimper, because this is beyond my wildest dreams. Having him back is already more than I could've ever hoped for, but to have him like this, too?

"Tell me." This time, his voice takes on a more pleading tone. Because that's James: always wanting to please me. Take care of me. Make sure I'm happy and my needs are met above anyone else's.

And it's never been like that with anyone else. It's always about the good of the many. Even before I became the Chosen Protector, I've never been allowed to pick what life to lead for myself. The Magicks Shoppe. Witch lessons. Not being allowed to leave Salem. Everyone else in my life only ever spoke of my duty to the world around me.

Not James. No, he's always been one to think of how to make my life easier, happier. Better.

Gods, I love him.

"Well, I thought a lot about us in here. I'd... turn off the lights. Use my powers to make the ceiling look like the night sky. And then just..." I sigh, closing my eyes. "Let go. Think of us in a better place. A different timeline where things didn't go to shit."

James places a reassuring kiss on my shoulder.

"Most of the time, it wasn't anything sexual," I admit. "Mostly, I dreamed of a life together. What our lives should've been had our future not been ripped away from us. But when I wasn't thinking of things like that, I fantasized about something more..."

"More what, baby?" he presses, his voice gravelly.

"Just... *More.*"

I feel his crooked smile against my neck, then a small bite

on my skin before he soothes it with the flick of his tongue. The danger of his sharp fangs turns me on even more for some reason. I know it goes against everything I was raised to believe in, but I almost beg for him to bite me.

To claim me.

To taste me.

I just want to surrender myself over to him.

When I moan at the thought, he laughs darkly.

One of his hands dips below the water, moving up my inner thigh in a slow, tantalizing caress. I lean back into him with a moan when his fingers reach my clit. Begin to circle it in a way that makes me hate him and love him at the same time.

"*James.*"

"Tell me, baby," he murmurs in my ear. "Did you ever imagine this? Did you imagine me playing with your pussy right here?"

I gasp for breath when his fingers finally come over my clit, rubbing it in a perfect, consistent, yet torturous rhythm. "Yes," I burst. "Yes, so many times."

His laugh is dark when he moves his index and middle finger down to my folds, where I'm slick and wet, and I'm not talking about the bath water.

"I've dreamt about this pussy countless times," he confesses. "How you would feel in my mouth. How you would *taste*. How I would happily spend hours worshipping at your fucking feet, eating you out for as long as you'll let me."

My chest rises and falls, my breathing embarrassingly fast and desperate, as if I've been drowning for months without him. And haven't I, though? Haven't I been practically anoxic this entire time?

He moves his two fingers lower, tapping at my entrance in a silent request for permission.

I don't hesitate to nod. *Enthusiastically.*

James growls and bites my earlobe before hooking both fingers into me, pushing through without further delay. It's almost forceful, but I love it. I'm already sore from earlier this morning, aching from the friction of his thick cock and everything we've done over the past twenty-four hours, but it's good. I like the pain. It serves as a reminder that he's real. That *this* is real and that my hallucinations haven't gotten the better of me. That the way he thrusts and hooks his fingers into me right now, the heel of his hand expertly pressed against my clit, isn't just another scene from the catalogue of fantasies in my head.

It doesn't take long before his fingers get me there. After too short a moment, I'm coming in his arms as he whispers impossible words.

...most incredible thing I've ever seen in my life...

...wanna come on your tits and face and just—

...have loved you since the second I laid eyes on you and can't believe...

I don't catch all of it—just bits and pieces through brief moments of consciousness as I come down from my orgasm.

With delicate movements, his hard cock a steel rod against my lower back, James pulls his fingers from my pussy and brings them to his mouth.

It's filthy and devastatingly hot.

"You okay?" he asks.

I cannot open my eyes for anything, so blissed out I can barely move. Somehow, though, I manage to nod.

"You taste amazing, by the way." He places open mouthed kisses on my skin, sucking at my neck and shoulder. "Hmmm, but I'd bet you taste better straight from the source."

"Huh? What are you—"

Even though I'm the Chosen Protector, and I should have better instincts than that, he manages to pick me up and place me on the edge of the tub, my back pressed against the cold tile, before I even know what's happening.

"Spread your legs," he orders, kneeling in front of me in the hot water. "I need to taste you again."

"But I—*Gods*." I fall back on the heels of my hands, my head lolling against the wall, as his tongue swipes me from the very bottom—so close to that tight ring of muscles—to my clit. It's there where he groans like a man starved, sucking and twirling his tongue as I call out his name, two fingers sunk deep inside me. One of my hands slips into his light hair, grasping, pulling. Holding on for dear fucking life because this man—

Oh, gods—

This man is going to kill me, and it won't be because he's a vampire.

"*James!*" I come harder than I ever have before, his tight grip on my hips and thigh only adding to the myriad of sensations his incredible mouth was able to produce.

My pussy pulses over and over again, squeezing his fingers through my release. And I'm so thankful for them. So thankful for this out-of-body experience that has me gasping for air as if I were on the verge of death.

And I love it.

I love him.

"I love you, too," he whispers into the crease of my thigh while I come down from my high. "I've never known something this powerful. I never want to give you up, no matter what we are in this fucked up world."

I open my eyes to look into his—concern and pain runs so deep in them. "I'm not leaving you."

"Even though I'm a..." He swallows thickly.

"No," I murmur, cupping his face, tilting it up toward mine as I bring my lips to his swollen ones. The kiss is soft, slow, and perfect. I can taste myself on his tongue, but it just serves as a reminder of what he did and how perfect we are together. "Nothing will keep us apart. Not if I can help it."

EPILOGUE

"It's really quite simple," I say, the heel of my favorite boots pressing down a little harder on the vamp's neck. "You either tell me who's been providing you with the guns, or we end this right here, right now."

"Cate, love," James interrupts my interrogation. "I don't mean to question your methods or anything—"

"Then don't," I retort with a raised brow.

He ignores me. "But don't you think it might be a bit difficult for the guy to reply when you're crushing his windpipe?"

I look down at the vampire who, were he not dead already, would probably already be due to suffocation. With a sigh, I release a little pressure—just enough so he can respond.

"Noah Cooke!" The vampire stutters. "Noah Cooke is the one who put us in touch with the arms dealer."

"The mayoral candidate?" I gasp. "That *fucker*!"

"Please. I told you the truth. Please let me go so I can get the hell out of here before they find out I told you. They'll kill me if—"

"Don't worry. They're not gonna kill you, because I am."

It doesn't take more than a second before I use a Fireball spell to burn him alive.

"That was..." James trails off.

Suddenly feeling very self-conscious, I walk over slowly to him. "I'm so sorry. Did that scare you? He was just never going to stop, and I couldn't risk him—"

"Hot. It was hot." James wraps me in his arms under the crescent moon, and, as he so often does, kisses me right on the jugular.

My entire body shivers at his fangs' closeness. It would just take him biting me a bit, a slight release of his venom, and—

"Did you just—Did you just moan from a *hug*?" He laughs.

I want to die of embarrassment.

"Not exactly," I say, pushing him away. "Was just... thinking about something."

It's been almost two weeks since we last talked about the possibility of me turning. He's given me space, and I appreciate it more than he knows. In that time, I've done more research on the matter as we've uncovered more and more secrets The Society and some accomplice vampires have volunteered.

"...Something?"

"About the possibility of me turning. You know, once it's done, it's done. We can't go back. You won't be able to get rid of me."

He takes hold of one of my hips with one arm, cups my face with the other. "Is that what you're concerned about? That we'll have gone through this big change only for me to change my mind?"

"Maybe? Or at least it's one of the concerns."

James nods, always so understanding. "It's a big deal, of

course. I'm not trying to downplay it, love. And while I would love for you to join me on this odd journey, I'm not going to try to convince you."

I sink into his arms, inhale the sweet scent of him. "That's just the thing, though. I don't need you to convince me. I already know I want to."

He gasps and pulls away. "Really?"

I bite my lower lip to keep from smiling too hard, but it's useless. "Really. I just... need to get my affairs in order, first. People to kill, evil politicians to stop. In the meantime, we can look for the vampires who chose to be good—there are bound to be some still around, underground. But just so you know, I'm yours. And I know you're mine. And I can't wait for you to turn me."

ACKNOWLEDGMENTS

Thank you to the epic books and TV shows who taught me to love this type of genre.

To Edward.

To Damon.

To Harvey.

To Spike.

And to all the girlies who love to spend hours debating all things Buffy, Twilight, and more.

<3

ABOUT THE AUTHOR

Caroline Frank is a Venezuelan indie author and self-proclaimed shoe addict. She currently resides in Philadelphia with her husband, two crazy cats, Señor Kitty and Salem, and her German Shepherd, Tilly.

She spends her days reading, crocheting, crafting, writing, and biking. Her favorite things include the first sip of an iced-cold Coke and using self-deprecating humor to get through the day.

Though she always planned to eventually take over the world, she thinks writing fun stories every day is pretty freaking awesome and plans to continue to do so for the foreseeable future.

ALSO BY
CAROLINE FRANK

<u>Seasons of Love Series (Open-Door Romantic Comedy):</u>

Fall Into You (Book 1)

Shall We Dance? (Book 2)

Happily Ever Disaster (Novella - Book 2.5)

Second Chance Snowmance (Book 3)

<u>Standalone:</u>

Reply All

www.ingramcontent.com/pod-product-compliance
Lightning Source LLC
Chambersburg PA
CBHW031547310726
48971CB00008B/2658

* 9 7 8 1 9 6 0 1 0 6 0 8 7 *